P9-DTS-080

Weekly Reader Books presents

# Mike Thaler

# IT'S ME, HIPPO!

pictures by

# Maxie Chambliss

## HARPER & ROW, PUBLISHERS

An I CAN READ Book ®

This book is a presentation of Weekly Reader
Books. Weekly Reader Books offers book clubs for
children from preschool through high school. For
further information write to: **Weekly Reader
Books,** 4343 Equity Drive, Columbus, Ohio 43228

Published by arrangement with Harper & Row,
Publishers, Inc.

It's me, Hippo!
Text copyright © 1983 by Mike Thaler
Illustrations copyright © 1983 by Maxie Chambliss
All rights reserved. No part of this book may be
used or reproduced in any manner whatsoever without
written permission except in the case of brief quotations
embodied in critical articles and reviews. Printed in
the United States of America. For information address
Harper & Row, Publishers, Inc., 10 East 53rd Street,
New York, N.Y. 10022. Published simultaneously in
Canada by Fitzhenry & Whiteside Limited, Toronto.
10 9 8 7 6 5 4 3 2 1
First Edition

Library of Congress Cataloging in Publication Data
Thaler, Mike, date
    It's me, Hippo!

    (An I can read book)
    Summary: With the help of his animal friends, Hippo
builds a house, paints a picture, breaks out in spots,
and celebrates a birthday.
    [1. Hippopotamus—Fiction.  2. Jungle animals—
Fiction]  I. Chambliss, Maxie, ill.  II. Title.
III. Series
PZ7.T3It 1983      [E]        82-48848
ISBN 0-06-026153-6
ISBN 0-06-026154-4 (lib. bdg.)

I Can Read Book is a registered trademark of
Harper & Row, Publishers, Inc.

For J.F.

to say it simply

*thanks*

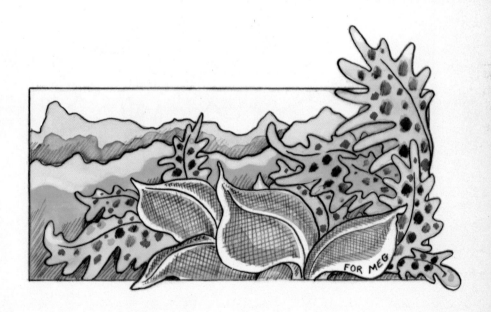

# Contents

# HIPPO MAKES A HOUSE

One morning Hippo was in the river.

He looked around.

"All my friends have houses,"

he thought.

"I would like a house too."

So he climbed out of the river

and walked to the store.

He bought a hammer, a saw, and a cap.

He put on his cap

and walked back to the jungle.

But Hippo did not know
how to make a house.
He sat down under a tree.
He was very sad.

Soon Parrot came by.

"What's the matter, Hippo?"

asked Parrot.

"I want to make a house,"

said Hippo,

"but I do not know how."

"Do not worry," said Parrot.

"I will help you."

And he began to gather twigs.

He took the twigs

to the top of a tree.

He piled them together

and made a nest.

"There is a house for you,"

said Parrot.

And he flew away.

11

Hippo looked up at his new house.

He slowly climbed the tree.

When he got to the top,

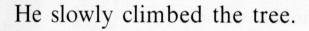

he jumped in the house.

*Crash!*

Hippo was on the ground.

His house was on his head.

"That is a nice hat," said Mole.

"It is not a hat, it is a house,"

said Hippo.

"That is not a house," said Mole.

"This is a house."

And he dug a big hole.

"There," said Mole.

He pointed into the hole.

"*That* is a house."

"Thank you, Mole," said Hippo.

He looked at his new house.

Then he jumped in

head first.

*Blump!*

Hippo tried to move.

But he was stuck in his house.

Just then Elephant walked by.

"What are you doing?" he asked.

"Hippo is moving into his new house,"
said Mole.

"That is not a house," said Elephant.

He pulled Hippo
out of the hole.

"Thank you, Elephant," said Hippo.

"That feels better.

But I still do not have a house.

And I do not know how to make one."

"I will tell you how to make a house,"

said Elephant.

"First, a house has to have

a strong floor."

"No, no," said Giraffe.

"First, a house has to have

a high roof."

"No, no," said Snake.

"First, a house has to be

long enough."

"Strong floor," said Elephant.

"High roof," said Giraffe.

"Long enough," said Snake.

"Strong!"

"High!"

"Long!"

Hippo laid down his

hammer and saw,

and walked away.

When he came to the river,

he jumped in.

He looked around.

The river was just his size.

It had a strong floor.

It was long enough.

And it had a roof as high as the sky.

Happily, Hippo splashed

around his house.

# HIPPO PAINTS A PICTURE

It was a beautiful morning.

Hippo rolled over in the river.

The sky was bright blue.

The sun was bright yellow.

"I think I will paint a picture,"

he said.

He climbed out of the river

and went to town.

He got some bright-yellow paint

and some bright-red paint.

He got some blue paint

and some white paint.

He got a canvas, a brush,

and a cap.

He put on his cap

and walked back

to the jungle.

He came to a big green field.

"This is perfect," he said.

He put down his canvas

and started to paint.

He painted all morning.

By lunchtime

he had a beautiful picture.

He stepped back to admire it.

He had painted the grass, the tree,

the mountains, the sky, and the sun.

"After lunch I will paint that flower.

Then my picture will be finished."

Hippo ran home to eat his lunch.

Then he ran back to the field.

He put some red paint on his brush

and painted the flower.

He stepped back.

"There." He smiled. "I am finished."

Snake wiggled up.

"It does not look finished to me,"

said Snake.

"You did not put in that cloud."

"It was not there this morning,"

said Hippo.

"Well, it is there now," said Snake.

"All right," said Hippo.

He put some white paint on his brush

and painted the cloud.

"There. *Now* it is done."

"Not quite," said Snake.

"A bird just landed on that tree."

"We can pretend we do not see him,"

said Hippo.

"But he is there," said Snake.

"All right, all right," said Hippo.

"I will put him in!"

Hippo painted the bird.

"There," he said.

"Now my painting is *perfect.*"

"Not quite," said Snake.

"Snake," said Hippo,

"I have painted the grass,

the flower, the tree,

the mountains, the sky, the sun,

the cloud, *and* the bird.

I do not see anything else to paint."

"Me," said Snake.

"You did not paint me."

And he wiggled right into the center

of the field.

"Come back here, Snake!" said Hippo.

"No!" said Snake.

"Please come here," begged Hippo.

"No!" said Snake.

"Come over here!" shouted Hippo
as loudly as he could.

Just then, Lion came by.

"What is all the noise?" he asked Snake.

"What is all the fuss about?"

asked Monkey and Mole.

"Do you need any help?"

asked Elephant.

"What is the matter?" asked Giraffe.

31

Hippo looked at everyone

standing in the middle of the field.

Then he looked at his painting.

"I give up," he said.

And he threw his brush into the air

and walked away.

"What's wrong with Hippo?"

asked Lion.

"His painting was giving him

a lot of trouble," said Snake.

"Let's look at it," said Giraffe.

So all the animals went around

to the other side of the canvas.

They looked at the painting.

Then they looked at the grass

and the flower,

the mountains and the sky,

the sun and the cloud,

the tree and the bird.

"I do not understand why Hippo

was having so much trouble,"

said Elephant.

"His painting looks perfect to me."

# HIPPO FEELS WONDERFUL!

Hippo opened his eyes.

The river felt good.

The sun felt good.

And he felt wonderful.

He hopped out of the river

and skipped off to find

one of his friends.

When he came

to Monkey's tree,

he shook it.

"Monkey," he called,

"it's me, Hippo.

Come down

and play."

Monkey poked out his head.

"I can't play with you," said Monkey.

"I am sick."

Hippo looked up.

Monkey was covered with red spots.

"Get well soon, Monkey," said Hippo.

"Drink a lot of banana juice."

"Poor Monkey," thought Hippo.

And he went down the road

to find Snake.

He tapped on Snake's log.

"Snake," he called, "it's me, Hippo.

Come out and play."

Snake stuck his head out.

"I can't play with you," said Snake.

"I am sick."

Hippo looked at both ends of Snake.

He was covered with red spots.

"Get well soon," said Hippo.

"And stay off your feet."

"Poor Snake," he thought.

He went down the road to find Elephant.

Elephant was sleeping under a tree.

"Yoo-hoo, Elephant!" shouted Hippo.

Elephant opened one eye.

"I am sick, Hippo.

I can't play with you."

Elephant pointed to the red spots

on his trunk.

"I hope you feel better soon,"

said Hippo.

"Stay out of drafts."

"I hope Giraffe is not sick too,"

said Hippo.

And he hurried

down the road.

But Giraffe *was* sick.

He had red spots

all over his neck.

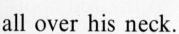

And Lion had them

all over his face.

And Parrot had them

all over his beak.

"Maybe Mole is okay," said Hippo.

And he ran to Mole's hole.

"Hello, Mole," called Hippo.

"How are you today?"

Mole stuck his head out.

His nose was covered with red spots.

"Get well fast," said Hippo.

"Gee, everybody is sick!" he said.

And he sadly started for home.

On his way he saw Monkey and Lion

and Elephant and Snake and Giraffe

and Parrot and even Mole.

They were playing cards together.

"I would love to play cards, too,"

said Hippo.

"Oh no, Hippo!" they all shouted.

"Do not come near us

or you will catch our red spots."

Hippo felt sad.

He went back to the river alone.

"Why do I have to be so well?"

he thought.

He sat and looked in the water.

Suddenly he saw something on his nose.

It was a red spot!

And there was another!

And another!

Hippo jumped up and down.

He ran back to his friends.

And they played cards

until they were all well.

49

# HIPPO'S BIRTHDAY

Hippo woke up bright and early.

It was a very special day.

Today was Hippo's birthday!

"Happy Birthday to me," said Hippo.

Hippo climbed out of the river

and hurried to the road.

Soon Monkey came skipping by.

"Hi, Monkey," said Hippo.

"Hello, Hippo," said Monkey.

"Do you know what today is?"
asked Hippo.

"Tuesday," said Monkey,
and he skipped away
down the road.

Then Snake came wiggling by.

"Hi, Snake," said Hippo.

"Hello, Hippo," said Snake.

"Do you know what special day

this is?" asked Hippo.

Snake thought for a moment.

"Sure I do.

It's National Snake Day."

And he wiggled off down the road.

Then Giraffe came trotting by.

"Hi, Giraffe," said Hippo.

"Hello, Hippo," said Giraffe.

"Do you know what very special day
this is?" asked Hippo.

"Nope," said Giraffe.

"Give me a hint."

"It is the perfect day
to have a party," said Hippo.

"Oh, Happy Valentine's Day?"
said Giraffe.

And he trotted away
down the road.

Hippo felt sad.

He started to walk back to the river.

Just then Elephant came by.

"Hello, Hippo," said Elephant.

"Hi," said Hippo.

"Why do you look so sad, Hippo?
Did you forget that today
is your *birthday*?"
shouted Elephant.

And out of the jungle

jumped Monkey and Snake and Mole

and Giraffe and Parrot and Lion.

They were all wearing party hats.

"SURPRISE!" they shouted.

"Oh, my," said Hippo.

Elephant put a party hat on Hippo.

They sang "Happy Birthday, Hippo"

and danced around him.

Then they took out Hippo's presents.

Hippo opened Giraffe's present first.

It was a very long scarf.

Hippo wrapped it around

and around his neck.

"I made it myself," said Giraffe.

"This will keep me very warm,"

said Hippo.

Next he opened
Monkey's present.
It was a swing.
"I love it!" said Hippo.
And he pretended to swing.

Next he opened Snake's present.
It was a very small stocking cap.
Hippo put it on top
of his party hat.
"It just fits," he said.

59

Parrot gave him a beautiful feather.

Hippo put it in his cap.

Then he opened Elephant's present.

It was a long wool tube.

"What is it?" asked Hippo.

"It's a nose warmer," said Elephant.

"Just what I wanted," said Hippo.

And he put it on his nose.

Then Mole and Lion gave him a basket

filled with his favorite foods.

"A picnic!" said Hippo.

"I love picnics!"

Hippo and his friends ate and sang
and danced until night.

Finally it was time to go home.

They each gave Hippo a hug

before they left.

He stood in the moonlight

and waved good-bye

to all his friends.

Then he patted his cap

and his nose warmer.

He threw the end of his scarf

over his shoulder.

And he skipped

all the way back

to the river.